The Paper Dragon

by Marguerite W. Davol

illustrated by Robert Sabuda

ATHENEUM BOOKS for YOUNG READERS

To the Western New England storytellers, whose tales have inspired me
— M. W. D.

In loving memory of my great-uncles, Winston F. Beach and Stanley L. Gutt
— R. S.

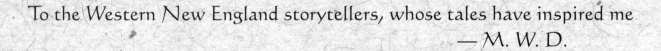

Atheneum Books for Young Readers
An imprint of Simon & Schuster Children's Publishing Division
1230 Avenue of the Americas
New York, New York 10020

Book design by Michael Nelson

Chinese characters rendered by Sui Cheung Tsang
The text of this book is set in Calligraphic 421.

Printed in Hong Kong
10 9 8 7 6

Library of Congress Cataloging-in-Publication Data
Davol, Marguerite W.
The paper dragon / by Marguerite W. Davol ; illustrated by Robert Sabuda.—1st ed.
p.   cm.
Summary: A humble artist agrees to confront the terrifying
dragon that threatens to destroy his village.
ISBN 0-689-31992-4
[1. Dragons—Fiction. 2. China—Fiction.] I. Sabuda, Robert, ill. II. Title.
PZ7.D32155Par 1997
[E]—dc20   95-32166

*Each picture has been cut from painted tissue paper created by the artist
and adhered to Japanese handmade Sugikawashi paper.*

WHAT THE CHINESE CHARACTERS STAND FOR

 Courage

 Loyalty

 Love

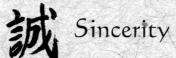 Sincerity

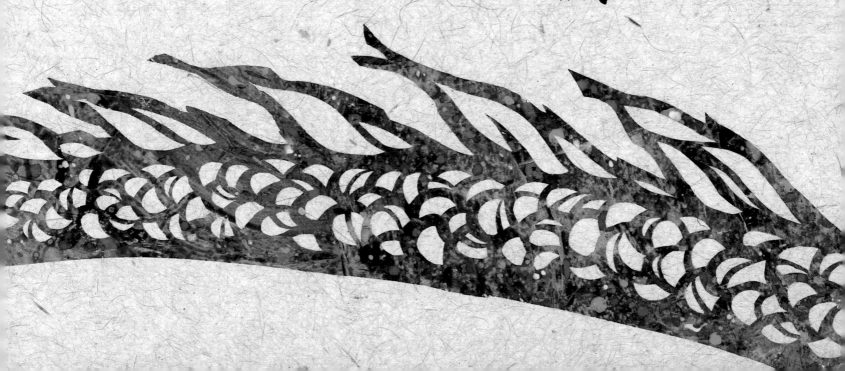

*L*ong, long ago, there lived a humble artist named Mi Fei. Between each day's sunrise and sunset, Mi Fei would dip his narrow brushes in colored inks and paint on paper scrolls. He loved to paint the glorious past — scenes of the gods and their festivals, portraits of great heroes and their deeds. People from far beyond his village came to buy Mi Fei's scrolls so they could learn about their gods and heroes as one would learn from books.

But the artist cared nothing for the fame his paintings brought him. He was a simple man, content to live and work in his own village. When children crowded his windows to watch him paint, Mi Fei would call to them, "Come in!" When neighbors appeared at his door, he put his brushes aside, ready to listen to their latest tale of triumph or woe. Mi Fei was happy, surrounded by people he loved.

One morning, Mi Fei's work was interrupted by shouts outside his window. "A messenger! A messenger!" people cried as they ran past. Brush in hand, Mi Fei rushed to join his neighbors in the village square. The messenger, Mu Wang, brought distressing news.

"The great dragon of Lung Mountain, Sui Jen, has awakened from its hundred years' sleep and is loose upon the land," the messenger gasped. "Its huge legs have trampled rice fields into mud, and the winds created by its lashing tail have uprooted the mulberry trees, destroying the silkworms. Sui Jen's fiery breath has scorched the tea leaves on the bushes. Villages everywhere are in ruins.

"Someone must face the dragon," Mu Wang warned the crowd. "Someone must convince it to sleep once more, or your village, too, will be crushed under the weight of Sui Jen."

The frightened people murmured among themselves. Was anyone in their village brave enough and clever enough to confront a dragon? One by one, they turned to Mi Fei. "You know all about gods and heroes," one of the villagers said. "Surely you can find a way to stop Sui Jen."

Mi Fei shook his head. "I am no hero," he protested, "only a simple artist who paints the past. All I know of heroic deeds has been told to me by others!" But the villagers crowded around him, pleading for his help. Looking into their worried faces, he knew he could not refuse.

The next morning Mi Fei tucked some rice cakes into his pack, along with brushes, paper, and ink. He bundled up his painted scrolls to bring him comfort. Knowing he might never see friends and neighbors again, Mi Fei looked around his beloved village one last time. Then he sadly set off for Lung Mountain.

Through valleys and across streams Mi Fei walked, stopping only to pick a few berries to eat or to quench his thirst at a spring. After many hours, he reached Lung Mountain. Mi Fei stared upward. Smoke and flames billowed from the mountaintop, and enormous rocks bounced down the steep slopes. Mi Fei was frightened, but up, up he climbed, until he stood at Lung Mountain's peak. Thick mist swirled around him.

Then through the mist, with a rumbling roar so loud Mi Fei thought his head would burst, the dragon appeared. "Hah, who dares to disturb Sui Jen, the source of fire, the heart of the mountain?"

Mi Fei trembled. He turned to run away from the terrifying sight. But the worried faces of the villagers filled his mind and Mi Fei turned back to face the dragon. He bowed low and managed to say, "I am Mi Fei, a humble painter of scrolls."

Bright fire spurted from the dragon's nostrils, hot on Mi Fei's face. The wind from its lashing tail nearly blew him off his feet, but somehow Mi Fei was able to stand his ground.

"Please, Sui Jen, the villages below are in ruins. You have scorched the tea leaves and trampled the rice, leaving nothing for people to eat or drink. You have uprooted the mulberry trees and the silkworms are dying, leaving nothing for people to wear or sell. I beg of you, return to your sleep of a hundred years."

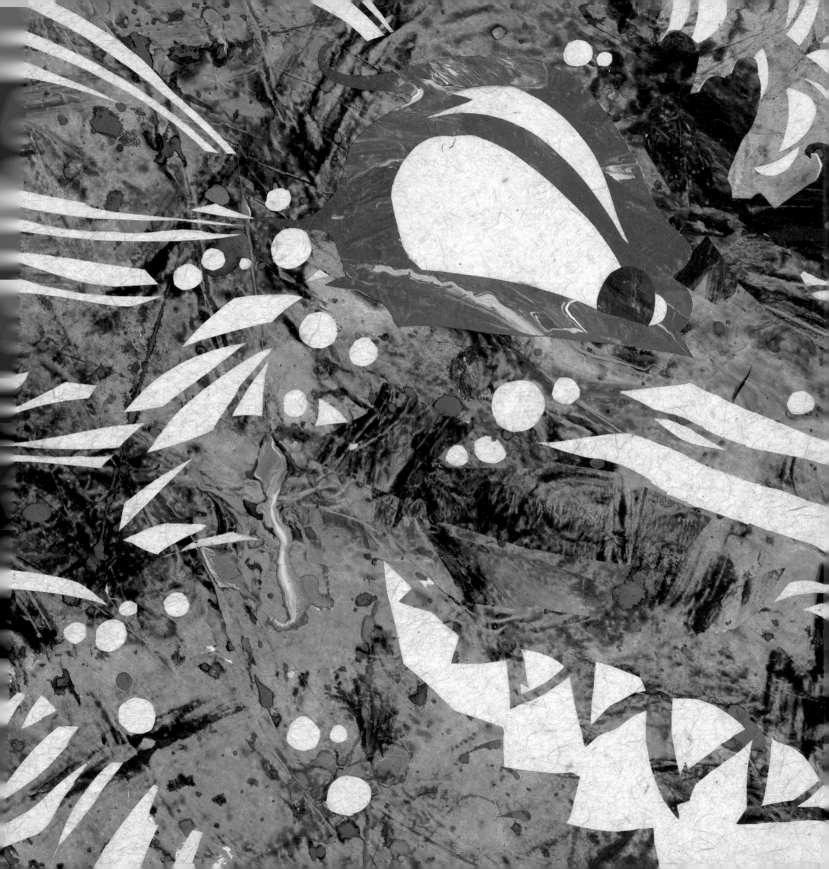

Huge scales glistened as the dragon coiled itself into a tight circle. Its red eyes glowed. "Hah, Mi Fei, know that before I return to my ageless slumber, someone must perform three tasks. Until then," thundered the dragon, its forked tongue flicking in and out, "I must prowl the countryside, trampling and burning all in my path."

Mi Fei sighed. Could a simple artist stop Sui Jen's devastation? His voice very small, Mi Fei asked the dragon, "What . . . what are the three tasks?"

Sui Jen's terrible teeth clicked once, twice. "First tell me, Mi Fei," the beast said, "what is the most important thing your people have created?"

The artist answered without thinking. "Paper," he said. "The paper on which I paint my scenes."

"Paper? Indeed!" The dragon howled with laughter. "The first task, then, is to bring me fire — wrapped in paper. Go. Do this before sunset or I must devour you."

Mi Fei crouched behind a large rock, seeking shelter from the dragon. He shook his head. "How can I carry out Sui Jen's task?" he said to himself. "Impossible! I was foolish to say paper, important as it is to me, instead of brass. Or tin. But paper . . ."

Mi Fei looked down at the bundle of scrolls he had carried from his village. People far and wide learn of their history from my paper scrolls, he thought. Perhaps knowing about the past can help me find answers for the present.

Mi Fei unrolled one scroll after another, looking at each of them carefully. On one scroll, he had painted a celebration of light, the Festival of the First Full Moon. Mi Fei smiled as he examined the scene. Then he took out his small knife and cut the paper scroll, folding and fashioning it into a different shape.

Before the sun slid from sight, Mi Fei returned to face Sui Jen. Although nervous so close to the dragon, he took a candle stump from his pack and lit the wick from Sui Jen's fiery breath. Mi Fei placed the burning candle inside the paper lantern he had made. The dragon laughed and the flame in its nostrils died to a wisp of smoke. Mi Fei knew he had succeeded.

But then Sui Jen began to whip its heavy tail back and forth so violently that the clouds in the sky were swept away. "Your second task is to bring me the wind captured by paper," the dragon roared. "Do this before noon tomorrow or I must devour you."

Mi Fei slept very little that night. He had solved the first task, but the second seemed far more difficult. "Can my scrolls help me again?" he asked himself over and over. In morning's orange glow, he again unrolled his scrolls, one after another. Mi Fei stared at one, a hero's rescue of a beautiful princess lost in the hot desert, then nodded. Quickly he took out his small knife and cut the paper scroll, folding and fashioning it into a new shape.

Mi Fei found the dragon resting, its eyes closed. He approached the scaly beast and, with the folded paper, began to fan its face. The wind captured in the fan tickled Sui Jen. Opening its eyes, the dragon laughed once more and lazily uncoiled its massive tail. Mi Fei knew he had succeeded again.

But almost instantly, Sui Jen opened its red eyes wide and bellowed, "Your third task is to bring me the strongest thing in the world carried in paper. Do this before sundown or I must devour you."

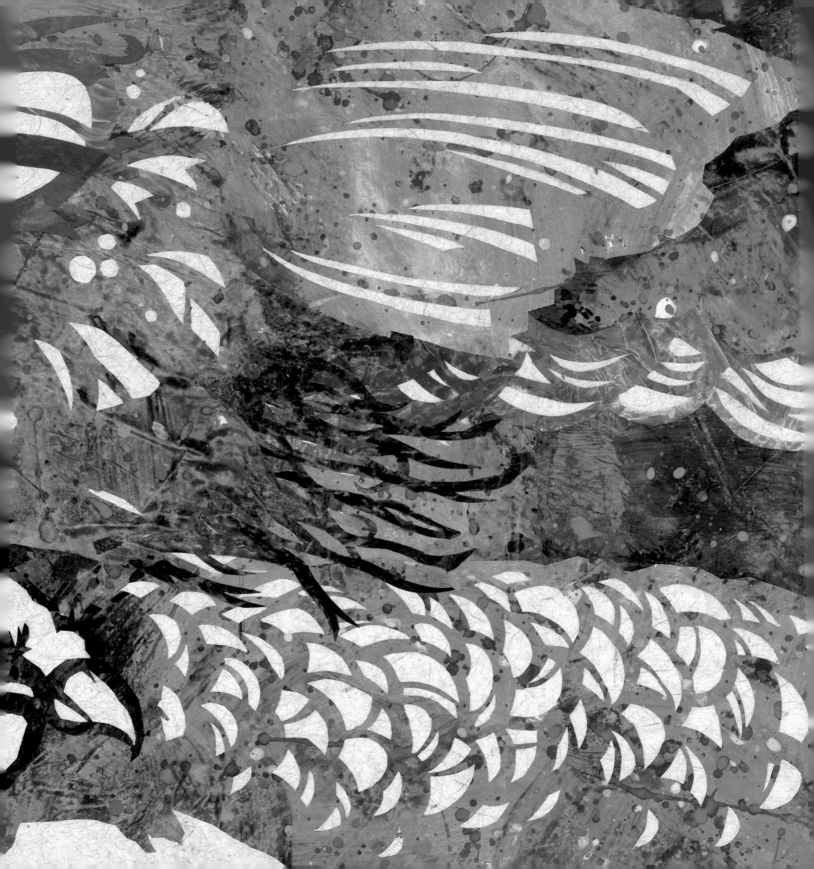

Mi Fei hurried back to the shelter of the rock. "The strongest thing in the world," he repeated. "Is it Sui Jen? Or the rock I now lean against? What huge, heavy thing can be carried in paper?"

His scrolls had saved him twice and Mi Fei once again unrolled each one, searching for an answer. But no matter how hard he looked, this time not one of the scrolls offered Mi Fei a solution. He set them aside, disheartened. "Surely Sui Jen will devour me at sundown," he said.

Resigned, Mi Fei reached into his pack and took out his brushes, paper, and inks. He began to paint, certain that it would be for the last time. But he did not paint scenes of gods or heroes. Instead, Mi Fei painted what was closest to his heart, what he cherished most. He began to paint the people of his village — young and old, men, women, and children.

Mi Fei worked until the sun arced low in the west, then wearily laid his brushes aside.

He looked at the familiar world he had re-created, the faces of friends and neighbors he loved. Words began to crowd his head, take shape, and become a poem. Mi Fei picked up his brush and made the poem a part of his painting.

When he had finished, Mi Fei looked for a long time at what he had created. Then he smiled and nodded. He knew what he would do. This time Mi Fei did not cut the paper or fold it into a new shape. Instead, he carefully rolled up the scroll and tied it with a red ribbon.

英 忠

Once more Mi Fei trudged along the narrow mountain path. The enormous beast lay waiting, its great length coiled around and around the mountaintop. Opening its wide mouth lined with pointed yellow teeth, the dragon said, "Well, am I to eat you for dinner?"

Mi Fei held out the picture he had created and said in a clear, firm voice:

Love can move mountains,
Stretch the sky, calm the sea.
Love brings light and life.

愛 誠

英

忠

When he had finished, Mi Fei looked into Sui Jen's eyes. He was astonished to see that the dragon was shrinking. In a whisper rather than a roar, Sui Jen said, "Thank you, Mi Fei. You have found the way for me to sleep once more. Truly, the strongest thing in the world is love."

With that, the dragon became smaller and smaller until, with a flip of its tail, Sui Jen disappeared. In its place, Mi Fei found a small paper dragon. He carefully placed it within the scroll to take back to his village.

愛

誠

For the rest of his long life, Mi Fei continued to paint the gods and their festivals, to portray the exploits of great heroes. He continued to paint portraits of the villagers he knew and loved. But whatever he painted, he always drew a small dragon in one corner to remind everyone of the strongest thing in the world.